DINO DETECTIVE
AND
AWESOME POSSUM

PRIVATE EYES

THE CASE OF THE MISSING SOCKS

by Tadgh Bentley

Penguin Workshop

For Fionn, again and always

PENGUIN WORKSHOP
An Imprint of Penguin Random House LLC, New York

Copyright © 2021 by Penguin Random House LLC. All rights reserved. Published by Penguin Workshop, an imprint of Penguin Random House LLC, New York. PENGUIN and PENGUIN WORKSHOP are trademarks of Penguin Books Ltd, and the W colophon is a registered trademark of Penguin Random House LLC. Manufactured in China.

Visit us online at www.penguinrandomhouse.com.

Library of Congress Cataloging-in-Publication Data is available upon request.

ISBN 9780593093528 (paperback)   10 9 8 7 6 5 4 3 2 1
ISBN 9780593093511 (library binding)   10 9 8 7 6 5 4 3 2 1

CHAPTER ONE
MISSING SOCKS

NOOOOOO!!!

It was a lovely morning in Berp. The sun had just risen, birds flew from branch to branch, and the postman was on his morning rounds…

… when suddenly, a loud howl pierced the calm of the morning.

"Noooooo!!!"

It was Awesome Possum.

"Dino! My sock! My Butch Malone sock! It's missing!"

Plant watched from the windowsill as Dino rushed to Possum's side. "Another one?"

"This isn't just another one, Dino! I saved cereal box tokens for five weeks to get these socks. I've worn them so much that one had a giant hole in it."

Losing socks wasn't normally a big thing—it happened every once in a while. But recently, the problem had been getting worse. At first it had been one or two a week. Now socks were disappearing so often that they couldn't keep count.

For Dino, it wasn't a big deal. If one sock was missing, she just mixed and matched. It was a great opportunity to try some fresh new looks.

For Possum, it was a different story. He wasn't the kind of possum that walked around in odd socks. He liked his socks matching, thank you very much. The good thing was that, usually, pairing matching socks wasn't a problem.

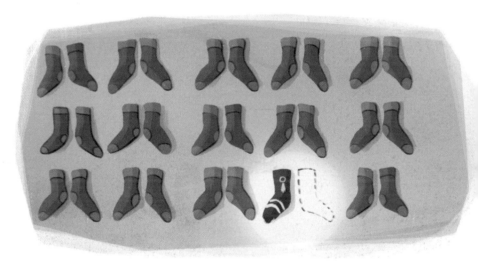

But now the worst had happened. The one pair that was different, his *favorite* Butch Malone socks… one was missing.

Possum had seen the commercials on TV. Special, limited edition Butch Malone socks, said to be worn by the great man himself.

"This is bad, Dino. Really bad."

"We'll find it, Possum. It can't have gone far."

They checked all over their bedroom.
They checked under the beds and on top
of wardrobes, in closets and in drawers.
But they found only what Possum
already knew:

Nothing. The sock was gone.

"Something is strange here, Dino," said
Possum. "I can smell it."

"Oh," said Dino, slightly embarrassed.
"That might be my feet. I've been wearing
these socks for four days in a row now."

Never mind the smell, Possum thought.
This sounds like a case for:

DINO DETECTIVE
AND
AWESOME POSSUM,
PRIVATE EYES

Sigh.

CHAPTER TWO

DATA ANALYSIS

Dino and Possum searched for a pattern. The socks that were missing: Were they a particular color, material, or size? *When* had they gone missing? Was it on a particular day of the week, or at a certain time of day? Were other people's socks missing, too?

It turned out that socks of every type and color were missing. There were left socks and right socks, short socks and long socks. They went missing on random days of the week, and from different places throughout the house.

Possum sighed and turned to his sister. "Is it just *our* socks? Or does this case go bigger?"

Possum had been on the lookout for the next Big Case for a while, the case that would finally put the agency on the map. They had been working a few small-time cases recently. The mystery of Samuel Crokus's missing homework? Easy. Who framed Trogdor for unicycle theft? That was simple, too.

But now it seemed like a case was falling right into Possum's lap like a giant pile of dirty socks. Their socks. Gone. Stolen in the night by some fiend, some criminal. Who knew what could be happening to them? Who knew the mind of the thief? Maybe they would get a ransom note soon. Maybe they would see their socks on TV on the feet of a masked villain. Possum's eyes lit up as he realized that this had all the trappings of a Big Case...

… But the investigation was halted by Dad's voice booming from downstairs. "Possum! Dino! You're going to be late for school! Come down and have some breakfast!"

Unlike Dino, Possum thought that breakfast was an unnecessary distraction. But the list of people who knew about their socks was short. Perhaps they needed to speak to witnesses...

Possum and Dino headed downstairs with Plant. "Dad, have you been missing any socks recently?" asked Dino.

Dad didn't look up from his paper. "Missing socks? Sure! Socks go missing all the time; it's no great mystery." He chuckled and continued reading.

"But more and more socks are missing!" said Possum. "If this continues, I—"

"If this continues, you're going to be late for school," said Dad. "Eat your breakfast and get ready for the bus."

Next, Dino and Possum asked Mom. No dice. Just like Dad, she didn't want to

talk about missing socks, either. "They must be somewhere, Dino. Socks don't grow legs and walk off. You need to be more careful with your things. Now get yourselves ready for school!"

"But, Mom, we're on a Big Case! This is a serious investi—"

"Well, you can take your Serious Investigation to SCHOOL!"

The only other person who might know something about their socks was Grandma Thunderclaps, but she had just left for a knitting conference that morning.

With no other witnesses to speak to, Dino and Possum trudged out the door as the school bus pulled up.

I still don't know why they feel the need to bring me to school every day.

"No one is taking this problem seriously, Dino," said Possum. "You know what that means?"

"That they are all in on it, and trying to throw us off the scent?"

"What? No! It means that we're on our own. But what do we do? We have no clues, no witnesses, no leads."

"We need more information," sighed Dino. "I'll talk to kids at school, find out just how big this laundry load is. Someone out there *must* know something. What about you?"

"Me?" said Possum. "I'm going to the Brain Trust."

Dino rolled her eyes as she headed to the back seat of the bus.

CHAPTER THREE

THE BRAIN TRUST

The Brain Trust. A crack team of (amateur) private investigators. Possum looked around at the other members of the group: Roland and Olivia. Every day they met up at HQ (the monkey bars) to swap notes and talk about their lives as (amateur) private detectives.

Everyone had their own cases they were working. Olivia had just wrapped up a big Halloween candy bust.

Roland was just finishing up his presentation on the McCluskey case. "... So it turns out that the team of international pasta assassins really *was* in his head the whole time. It was just his brother eating his dinner!"

"What about you, Possum? You still waiting for that Big Case?" asked Olivia.

Possum's turn. "Anyone notice anything unusual about their socks?"

Roland and Olivia both looked down at their feet, then blankly at Possum.

"You still got all your socks?" asked Possum.

"Where would our socks have gone?" asked Roland.

"I don't know, Roland. That's the point. But are you missing any?"

"Well, of course. *Everyone's* missing socks," said Roland.

"*Everyone* is missing socks?" The problem was bigger than Possum had first thought. "How many socks have you lost?"

"Oh, I don't really keep track," Roland replied.

"Because you've lost so many?"

"What? No. It only happens sometimes. I could count on the toes of one hoof the number of socks I'm missing."

But Possum wasn't going to give up so easily. "Don't you think that's strange? That socks go missing and there has been no investigation? No police reports? No sock hunt?"

"Well, it's not *that* strange. Happens all the time, so I suppose people just get used to it. No one cares why. Socks just vanish."

So it's a mystery, thought Possum. A mystery that their agency could solve. But he needed some leads. "You got any ideas about where the socks go?"

"Butch Malone always says that

usually the simplest explanation is the most likely," said Olivia. "It's a part of his code. This one time, he was investigating a case where a guy thought that his wallet had been stolen by his brother's butler's friend's nephew's old teacher, who stole it to grow his French wallet collection that had been left to him by his old aunt. Turned out he had left it in his car."

"Socks just get blown off the clothesline," said Roland. "Simple."

"What about people who put their socks in the *dryer*?" asked Possum.

"Sucked into the pipes."

There was a pause. Possum had to admit that Olivia and Roland made a lot of sense, but it didn't explain why he and Dino were missing so many of *their* socks. If it was something that happened during washing, why wouldn't Mom's and Dad's socks be missing, too?

Possum needed more information.

CHAPTER FOUR
SCHOOL

Dino loved school, but today, it was hard to focus. Everywhere she looked brought her mind back to the Big Case.

Math.

English.

Even science.

SCIENCE
SOCKS
IN SPACE

DO ASTRONAUTS
WEAR SOCKS
MOON WALK?

POETRY
An ode to
Socks
By William Wordbinder

Oh, thou holy socks
By thy must I know thee
and the soft squishiness
of thine fluffy embrace.

+ –
× ÷
MATH
PROBLEMS
× ÷
+ –

1. A centipede loses
27 socks. How many
does she have left?

Dino had to find out just how big this crime wave was: Were they really the only ones being targeted? She considered setting up a shuttered office, a spotlight, and a lie detector, but thought that might send the wrong message.

Better to keep things light.

No one was missing any more socks than usual, but everyone had the odd sock vanish from time to time. And *they all* had a theory of what had happened to them.

Like Roland, most people thought that socks either blew off the clothesline or were eaten every now and then by the washing machine or the dryer (usually the dryer). No one could explain how or why a machine would eat a piece of clothing, but people seemed to believe it, anyway.

Why do socks even *need* washing? Plants love water *way* more than socks do.

There were lots of other ideas.

Despite what Dino's mother had told her, Staunton was sure that socks actually DO grow legs and walk off.

Clifford thought they were beamed up by aliens.

Melanie thought that socks actually *were* aliens, and that every now and then they had to return home.

Toots McGraw muttered something about gnomes, the Maxford twins thought that mice stole them to make sleeping bags, and Harold thought that Bigfoot used them to make fingers for his gloves.

Beatrice argued that Bigfoot didn't even wear gloves. Giant centipedes, on the other hand...

And on it went...

CHAPTER FIVE
THE SIMPLEST EXPLANATION

When Possum and Dino got home, they talked about what they had discovered during school. They had found more questions than answers.

Why were only *their* socks missing more than usual? Was there something special about them? Did they have some kind of magical property that allowed them to fly through windows? Perhaps they were fitted with a homing device that, when activated, sent them flying to some faraway land.

They made a list of the different theories Dino had heard at recess. Did any seem more likely than the others? Was there a pattern?

"I don't know, Dino. There are a lot of ideas here, and some of them are pretty crazy. The Loch Ness monster's uncle using them as sleeping bags for his pet fish?" Possum remembered what Olivia had said earlier. "Butch Malone always says that the simplest explanation is most likely the right one. These ideas all sound pretty far-fetched."

Dino's eyes darted from one idea to the next.

Aliens. Sasquatch. Mice.

"It seems most likely that it's some kind of thief. That's a pretty simple explanation," Dino replied.

"Okay, but how does that help us? Even if it is a thief, which thief is it? What's their motive? We still don't know why they are taking *our* socks and not anyone else's."

Dino thought back to an old *Butch Malone* episode.

A cereal thief is on the loose in the Big City. People coming down to breakfast discover that their Sugar Pops, Coco Crumbles, and Corn Crackers are all gone, and nobody can catch the culprit.

A CEREAL SHORTAGE PLAGUES THE CITY. PRICES ARE SKY-HIGH, AND PROTESTORS TAKE TO THE STREETS.

BUT BUTCH MALONE IS ON THE CASE.

HE HATCHES AN INGENIOUS PLAN: GATHERING WHAT CEREAL REMAINS, HE PLACES IT IN A HUGE BOWL WITH MILK, IN A WAREHOUSE JUST ON THE OUTSKIRTS OF TOWN.

"That's it!" said Dino.

"That's what?"

"We set a trap, and we catch them in the act. Rather than look for the thief, we let the thief come to us."

CHAPTER SIX
THE TRAP

> You know...I'm really more of a *day* plant.

As the sun set, a hush fell over the house, and the hums of day were replaced by the squawks of night. Possum and Dino looked over at the giant pile in the yard. It held all of their remaining socks. Socks of every color, pattern, and size.

Dino shuffled nervously from foot to foot. "Possum, I think I'm getting cold feet."

Possum looked down. "You should have saved a pair, Dino. We could be out here for a while."

"No, I mean *cold feet*. I'm not sure this is a good idea."

"This was *your* idea, Dino! We can't back out now."

"It was my idea to *trap* the thief. I didn't say anything about risking every sock we own in the process! What if we lose them all? I can't wear sandals in December!"

"It's a risk we have to take. A big sock pile like that? We'll have every sock thief from here to the Big City sniffing around."

Dino didn't like it, but Possum was right. This was the best chance they had at catching the thief.

Just as they had practiced, they recited their lines.

"Oh, I'm so tired," called Possum loudly to the night. "I have to go to bed immediately. Too bad we have to leave this giant pile of SOCKS out in the open. But never mind."

"What a shame! We'll have to go inside and leave all these SOCKS ALL ALONE for a whole night!" shouted Dino.

"Quite," Possum replied.

"Indeed," Dino said.

Dino and Possum stomped loudly toward the back door of the house…

…then dived into the nearest bush to watch and wait.

Watching and waiting…finally something I'm good at.

The night was long, cold, and horribly lacking in snacks. Possum's eyelids grew heavy as Dino fought the loud rumbling of her stomach, which she worried would give them away.

Time ticked on as tired eyes watched over moonlit socks.

Watching.

And waiting.

Dino bit her lip. "So, uh, Possum… what's the plan when the thief actually shows up?"

"We get a picture of them during the act. We take the photo to the police, who lock them up. We'll have cracked the Big Case, so we'll get our names in every detective paper in town. That's the way it works in *Butch Malone*."

"Can't we just grab 'em? That would be a lot simpler."

"No, Dino! We need *evidence*!"

"But why do you have *that* old thing? I thought you want us to be taken *seriously*." She pointed at the camera in Possum's hands.

To get the photo, of course. Finding a good camera had been a problem, and these were desperate times.

A rustle came from the bushes.

Dino and Possum watched as a fuzzy figure appeared, tiptoeing through the shadows. It barely made a sound as it moved from bush to bush. Possum was ready. Ready to take the photo that would crack this case wide open and send the (amateur) agency toward professional detective glory!

The figure paused in the darkness.

As it approached the socks, Possum held up the camera, and Dino prepared to spring.

The thief stepped into the moonlight.

"Stop right there!" shouted Possum.

Dino jumped into the yard, but quickly stopped dead in her tracks.

"Toots?" asked Dino. "What are *you* doing here?"

CHAPTER SEVEN

TOOTS MCGRAW

"**You're** the sock thief?!" Dino continued. "What have you done with his Butch Malone sock?!"

Toots stood frozen next to the sock pile, unsure what to do next. His long coat hung down in the still night.

Well, this is a new development.

Dino remembered her interview with Toots that morning. It was the first time she had spoken to him. He had a reputation for being… a little out there. Dino had seen Toots at band practice, but she had never seen him pick up an instrument. He was always hanging around on the edges of the recess field.

"You got it all wrong! I ain't your sock thief!" cried Toots.

"Then what are you doing here?" asked Possum.

"I've been watching you two!" cackled Toots. "Got a sock problem, don't ya? Heard you speaking at recess. Everyone thinks they know, don't they? But they don't know the truth! The terrifying truth! I know. Oh yes, I know. 'Cause the same thing is happening to me."

"Your socks are missing, too?" asked Possum.

"It's not my socks they're stealing, no." Toots paused to look both Possum and Dino squarely in the eye. "It's my underpants."

"Your *underpants*?!" cried Dino.

Toots nodded seriously. "They've been stealing my underpants for years. It was only a matter of time before they moved on to socks."

Dino couldn't believe it. This was bigger than she thought. "Who? Who is stealing them?"

Toots paused again. "It's the gnomes."

"Gnomes? Like… garden gnomes?" Possum asked.

"No! Not *garden* gnomes. That would be crazy. No. I'm talking about *underpants* gnomes. But now they're after your socks."

"Underpants gnomes?" asked Possum.

"That's right!"

"Who are now after our socks?" Dino added.

"That's what I'm telling ya."

Possum wasn't buying it. "I thought gnomes were supposed to be a friendly bunch," he said. "Always smiley, helpful in the garden, that sort of thing?"

"You're just not getting it, are ya!" cried Toots. "It's the perfect cover! Who would suspect sweet little gnomes of stealing your socks? 'Wouldn't harm a fly,' they say. 'Wouldn't do something like that,' they say. And all the while, they're racking up more undies than a shopkeeper in an underwear store."

Possum rubbed his brow. They had a Big Case to investigate, and this seemed a little far-fetched. "We've heard a lot of crazy ideas today, Toots. You got any proof?"

"No, I don't have any proof! These gnomes, they're clever, you see. Sneaky, too. They only steal them every now and then. They don't get greedy. They just—"

"If you don't have any proof, why should we believe you?" Possum interrupted.

"You don't have to believe *me*," said Toots. "Nobody ever believes me. But keep those socks out there, you'll see soon enough. You'll have all the proof you need."

CHAPTER EIGHT

GNOMES

Dino and Possum returned to their lookout spot while Toots took up Super Secret Hiding Space 2.

"This could be a lead, Possum!" said Dino excitedly.

Possum wasn't so sure. "I don't know, Dino. Butch Malone always says that the simplest explanation is usually the right one. Underpants-stealing gnomes who now have a taste for socks? It just sounds like another crazy idea to me."

I just don't understand why all of this has to happen *outside*. There's so much… *dirt* out here. No, thank you.

Possum and Dino settled back into the long task of watching the socks as Toots sat muttering to himself in the bush next to them. Plant struck up an awkward conversation with a mulberry bush, complaining about all the outside germs that were trying to get him.

"I'm hungry," whispered Dino. "It's been ages. I'm going for a snack."

But just then, something at the edge
of the lawn caught Possum's eye. Dark
shapes lurked in the bushes, rustling
through the shadows and the dim edges
of the lawn. Staying in the shadows, they
inched through the night, prowling their
way toward the sock pile.

Possum raised his camera. A few more
steps into the moonlight and he could
take the photo; then they could pounce.

But Toots wasn't waiting for the perfect photo opportunity. "Gotcha!" He dived out from his hiding place, lunging at the little figures.

The dark shapes froze at the sight of Toots running toward them.

But they didn't freeze for long.

Like a flash, they dashed across the lawn to the far end of the yard. Dino burst out of the bushes in hot pursuit. "Stop right there!"

When they got to the fence, one of the thieves quickly slid underneath the gap and into Mr. Thompson's yard, while the other two somersaulted high into the air, easily clearing the top.

Dino wasn't quite so dainty.

As she smashed through the fence, she got her first clear glimpse of the thieves as they scurried across the grass.

Toots was right.

They were gnomes. Tiny little men
with bushy beards and rosy cheeks that
wobbled underneath a black robber's
mask, their mouths set in a grizzled
frown. Their little legs were a blur as
they hurried across the yard, barely
slowed down by the giant bags they
carried on their backs. Even though they
were small, they were nimble and fast for
their size.

But Dino wasn't the school egg-and-spoon race champion for nothing. She gritted her teeth and raced on, gaining on them as they flew across the yard. Out of the corner of her eye she saw headlights come zooming around a corner.

A getaway car!

Dino was close to the slowest gnome, her feet clawing the ground as she ran. She made a desperate lunge…

Crash!

The gnome looked back and opened his mouth to laugh. But...

TWANG! His beard caught on the branches of Mr. Thompson's prize-winning Christmas tree.

The gnome lay dazed on the ground as the remaining thieves zipped and zoomed into the open car.

The doors slammed, the wheels kicked up dirt, and the car sped away into the night.

CHAPTER NINE

RADISHES

Dino, Possum, and Toots looked down at the gnome, whose rosy cheeks puffed in and out peacefully as he lay in the grass. He was out cold.

"Ha!" cried Toots. "I told you! Underpants gnomes!"

They looked down at the bag the gnome had been carrying. It was a large canvas sack, with somewhat suspicious markings. The bag had opened, and its contents had spilled out.

Underpants.

More underpants than a toddler on a monthlong vacation. Underpants of all shapes, sizes, and colors.

But what about the socks? They emptied out the bag fully. Not a single one.

"Hey, what's your problem, pal?" a squeaky voice called out. The gnome was awake.

"What's *my* problem?" responded
Dino. "What's *your* problem? Why are
you sniffing around our socks? And why
are you stealing people's underpants?"

"We're just borrowing them! They'll be
returned!"

"Returned? Why are you taking them
in the first place?"

"We have to." The gnome glanced up
sheepishly. "They're for the trolls."

"The trolls?" asked Toots.

"Why are you giving people's underpants to trolls?" asked Possum.

"Oh goodness, we're not *giving* them to the trolls. That would be ridiculous. Trolls are terrified of underpants."

"Then what use are they?!" cried Dino.

"To scare them away. They're stealing all our radishes."

Possum, Dino, and Toots looked blankly back at the gnome. "Your *radishes?*"

"Oh yes. Our radishes are the most delicious radishes one can find. The trolls can't get enough of them. We have to build scare-trolls to stop them."

"Scare-trolls?"

"Scare-trolls. They're like scarecrows, but made up only of underpants. We tried lots of things before—booby traps, catapults, decoys, fields full of jelly—but we found that underpants really are the most effect—"

"So you're telling me that you're stealing people's underpants to make scare-trolls that stop trolls from stealing your radishes?" asked Possum.

The gnome looked down at his little boots. "We prefer to say 'borrowed' rather than 'stole.' We return as many as we can, and we fix them up as good as new. Most times, people don't even know they've been missing. It's only occasionally that they get lost or ... eaten."

"But what were you doing around our socks?"

"We were searching. For underpants."

Possum and Dino looked at each other. This all sounded rather crazy and extremely complicated to them. Butch Malone always said that the simplest explanation was usually the best one...

... but what did the evidence say? The suspect had a bag full of underpants, and the explanation, while not very simple, sort of made sense.

The little gnome gathered his bag and everyone else's underpants and said his goodbyes. It was late, and he still had underwear to collect. "Can I please ask that you don't set traps for us poor unsuspecting gnomes? Big pile of clothes like that, we couldn't believe our luck. We thought there must be some underpants among all those socks."

The sock pile!

In the excitement of the chase, they had forgotten all about it. The thief could still be out there!

Dino, Possum, and Toots dashed
back through the yard, grass and leaves
kicking into the dark night air.

As they rounded the corner, Dino felt
her heart jump in her chest.

Every last one of the socks was gone.

FREE
SOCKS

Oh me, oh my.

CHAPTER TEN

THE THIEF

Dino resisted the urge to howl.

Possum blinked back hot tears.

How had they been so careless? They had left the socks all alone and now they had been snatched from under their noses.

Dino began thinking about a very cold-footed winter, when suddenly...
"Possum—look!" Lying in the open front doorway, shining in the moonlight...

"My missing sock! Although..." Possum went closer. It *looked* like his Butch Malone sock, all right, but *his* sock had a giant, frayed hole in it. This sock looked good as new.

Something else caught Possum's eye. Sitting inside the house on the kitchen table, lit by the moonlight that streamed in through the door, was a large canvas bag. *That wasn't there before*, thought Possum.

They crept into the house. Did this bag belong to the thief?

They opened it.

Socks. The bag was stuffed full of them. And not just any socks. They were all *their* socks. Dino recognized her multicolored rainbow socks and the socks she wore for salsa dancing, the socks that had been made into sock puppets, and her lucky socks. They were all there.

"But who would have brought them ba—"

A loud *THUNK* cut through the softness of the night.

Dino, Possum, and Toots froze. The noise had come from above, and now they heard footsteps clumping down the stairs.

"It could be the thief!" hissed Possum. "Hide!"

Possum readied the camera.

Toots slunk into the darkness.

Dino's mind raced with possibilities as the footsteps grew louder.

THUNK.

Who was this thief? Why were they taking their socks?

THUNK.

Was it a gnome? The gnome said they were only after underpants.

And the gnomes always *returned* underpants. They fixed them up, too.

THUNK.

Fixed them up?

Would someone…

… have fixed…

… their socks?

CHAPTER ELEVEN

It Was You!

Possum's eyes widened as it all became clear.

"Grandma! It was you this whole time!" he said.

"Goodness gracious, dears! What are you doing up so late?"

"Grandma!" cried Dino. "You're the one who's been taking our socks all along!"

"Well, of course, dears. I kept noticing more and more of them with giant holes. Couldn't have you going around with holey socks now, could we? I took them

Well, well, well. The big case cracks wide open.

to my knitting conference. Why were your other socks all outside?"

"We had to set a trap," Possum replied.

"A trap?"

"A trap. For a thief," said Possum.

"They were on a big case," added Toots.

"A big case?"

"But we caught some gnomes by mistake," continued Possum, "and then it turned out that they were actually taking people's underpants, not socks. And it was only to scare away trolls."

Grandma Thunderclaps looked down at them blankly, turned around, and thudded back up the steps.

Toots, Dino, and Possum stepped out into the cool night air. Darkness and quiet surrounded Berp. Somewhere, birds were softly calling into the shadows, children were fast asleep and snoring, and gnomes

were hunting for underpants.

"Well, I guess we owe you an apology, Toots," said Possum. "Underpants gnomes. Who would have thought it?"

Toots grinned. "See! Nobody believed me! But I was right all along!"

"You have to admit—underpants gnomes? It was all a bit… unlikely. But you cracked the case!" said Dino. "So, what's next?"

"Oh, this is just the beginning. You

heard the little fella. There's a whole bunch of trolls out there who are terrified of underpants. I'm going to find out why."

"Well, you know what they say—the simplest explanation is usually the best," Dino said. "Most of the time."

With that, Toots turned on his heel and left, scurrying into the moonlight.

Possum turned to Dino. "Well, Dino, it looks like our work here is done."

"For now, Possum." Dino yawned widely. "Time for bed. I have a feeling tomorrow will bring another case. Probably the big one."

Possum turned back toward the house, his mind spinning with possibilities. Another day lay ahead, and another case ready for...